For Heather – the rainbow after the rain
and for Sorrel, Emily and Hannah – H.R.

For Isabella, with love - Daddy

E-MAIL: JESUS@ANYTIME
by Hilary Robinson and Anthony Lewis

British Library Cataloguing in Publication Data
A catalogue record of this book is available
from the British Library.

ISBN: 0340 85537 1 (HB)
ISBN: 0340 855 38 X (PB)

First published 2003
10 9 8 7 6 5 4 3 2 1

Published by Hodder Children's Books,
a division of Hodder Headline Limited,
338 Euston Road, London, NW1 3BH

Printed in Hong Kong

e-mail: Jesus @ anytime

Hilary Robinson

Anthony Lewis

Hodder Children's Books

A division of Hodder Headline Limited

Let's imagine that Jesus
was teaching today.

Reports appear about a preacher who tells
amazing stories. With the help of twelve
friends He spreads the word about
God and love to many different people.

As His fame spreads, the media reveals Jesus can walk on water, turn water into wine and cure sick people.

He's hailed a hero.

a website announcing the arrival of the miracle man.

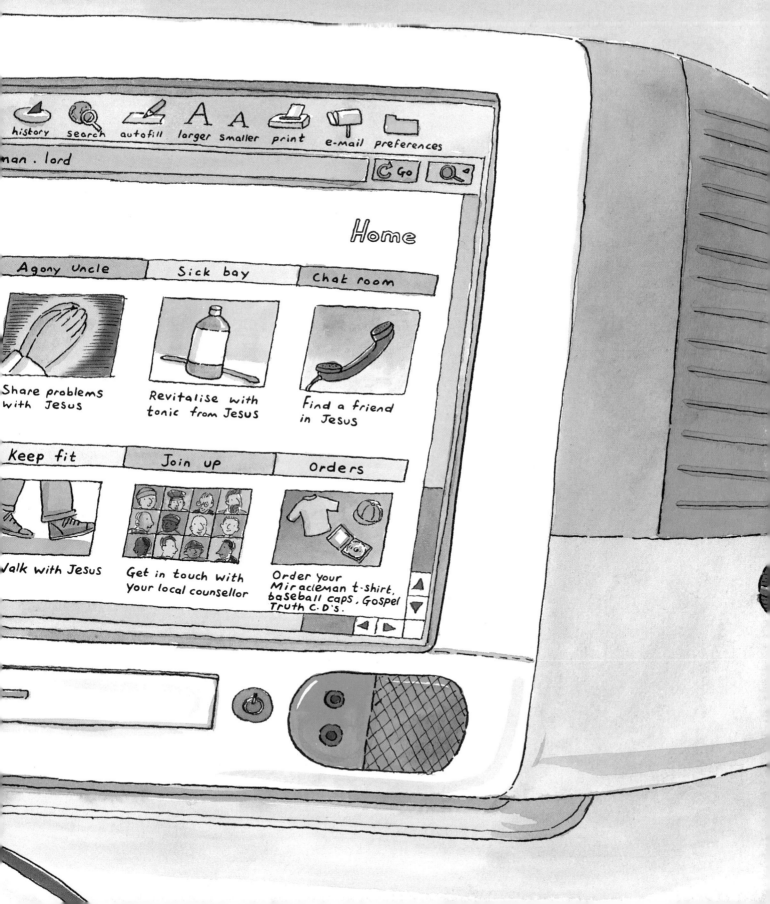

Followers of Jesus organise peace

rallies in every city of the world.

The Gospel Truth undertake a successful worldwide tour.

But good news turns bad when...

...the media seeks out Jesus.
They publish reports from false witnesses and
some people start to doubt the good things
that have been said about Him.

Some powerful people think Jesus is becoming too popular…

…and others say He must die.

Computer hackers send viruses
that destroy the website.

Even though Jesus dies many people
can't forget Him.

Four authors write true stories about His life.
They become bestsellers.

Now Christians all over

But we don't need websites and e-mails to chat

the world celebrate His life.

to Jesus today, because no matter where we are...

...He listens to us anytime.